Charlie
and the
Bullies

by **Sarah, Duchess of York**
Illustrated by Ian Cunliffe

Charlie and the Bullies

helping hand books

First published in Great Britain 2007 by Lloyds Pharmacy Ltd
Sapphire Court, Walsgrave Triangle, Coventry CV2 2TX
www.lloydspharmacy.com

In consultation with Cameron Wilson Ltd

Illustrated by Ian Cunliffe

'Ten Helpful Hints' contributed by Dr. Richard Woolfson,
child psychologist, Fellow of the British Psychological Society.

Printed in China

British Library Cataloguing in Publication Data
A catalogue record for this book is available from the British Library

ISBN 978-1-906260-09-5

All children face many new experiences as they grow up and helping them to understand and deal with each is one of the most demanding and rewarding things we do as parents. The helping hand books are for both children and parents to read, perhaps together. Each simple story describes a childhood experience and shows some of the ways in which to make it a positive one. I do hope these books encourage children and parents to talk about these sometimes difficult issues; talking together goes a long way to finding a solution.

Sarah

Sarah, Duchess of York

Charlie felt sick every morning as he made his way to school. It wasn't the lessons that worried him – he quite enjoyed those – it was the bits in between, particularly break time. Charlie was small for his age although he could run very fast but some of the older boys who were bigger decided to tease Charlie whenever they saw him.

Over time, the teasing had got worse and turned to pushing and shoving. One break time, one of the older boys, John, took it even further, pushing Charlie against a wall and punching him in the stomach when the teacher was not looking. Charlie wanted to fight back but he knew it was what John wanted and would only make things worse.

That evening, Charlie's
Mum saw his grazed knees
and bruises and asked him
how he had got them.

"We were playing around
in the playground,"
said Charlie, not
completely truthfully,
"and I fell over."

"Try to be more careful,"
said his Mum,
"you only have the one body."

Charlie desperately wanted to tell his Mum the
real reason why he had cuts and bruises, but he
felt that he would get into even more trouble if he
did. He thought it was his fault he was not liked
and that he had to solve it on his own.

The next day, Charlie's tummy really was sore but he said nothing and went to school. For the next few days, Charlie spent as much time as possible playing with lots of other children, so that he was always in a group. But, one morning, John and his friend Daniel got him on his own and started to push and tease him again. Choosing his moment, Charlie ducked between them and ran into the classroom where he put his head in his hands and sobbed.

A few minutes later, the door opened and in came Amy who sat next to Charlie in class.

"Hi Charlie!" said Amy but Charlie did not reply. "You've been crying, whatever's the matter?"

"Of course I have," said Charlie, "so would you if you were me." And then Charlie told Amy what  had been happening, ending with,

 "So there I am, too small and no use to anyone."

"You're a lot of use," said Amy. "You can run fast – and you're funny."

"Well, I don't feel funny, I'm miserable," said Charlie.

"Then you must tell your Mum and Dad."

"They wouldn't understand."

"Then I think you should tell Mrs Daventry."

"Tell me what?" said a voice from the door. They both turned to see Mrs Daventry, the form teacher, standing at the door.

"Nothing," said Charlie quickly, "nothing at all" and glared at Amy to keep quiet.

That evening, Charlie thought about what
Amy had said. He felt unable to tell his Dad. But
perhaps his Mum would listen.

"Mum," he said as he was eating his tea,
"if I tell you something, will you absolutely
promise not to tell Mrs Daventry?"

"Of course," said his Mum,
"you know you can tell Dad and me anything."

Charlie poured out his story to his Mum and, when he had finished, he cried, not because he was sad but because he was so relieved to have shared his problem. As his Mum comforted him, she said,

"I wish you had told me sooner, but together we can solve this. We just need a plan."

"Perhaps I should
fight back,"
said Charlie.

"No you should not!"
replied his Mum,
"You would be behaving just
as badly as they are and
that is just what they want."

They talked for a long time
and finally his Mum said,

"You will have to let me talk to Mrs Daventry
but I will do it quietly and make sure she says
nothing to John or Daniel."

Charlie was upset at first but then he decided to
trust his Mum – he always had and it had always
been the right thing to do.

Next morning though, he did not feel so brave and told his Mum he did not want to go to school.

"Yes you are," said his Mum, "with your head held high. I've spoken to Mrs Daventry and this is the day we start to solve this problem, together."

In class, Mrs Daventry told everyone about the project for next week and that Charlie would be the project leader. At break time, one of the teachers organised a game. Charlie joined in happily and forgot about his playground troubles for a little while.

That evening at home, Charlie found that his bedroom had been changed. All around the walls were the certificates and prizes that Charlie had won. Some of them were for little things, like the wrapper from the chocolate bar he'd won as a prize for painting when he was four.

"Maybe I am some use after all," he said to himself.

As the days went past, Charlie began to feel better about himself. He smiled more and walked tall which has nothing to do with anyone's height. The project was a great success and the children all voted for Charlie to be project leader again sometime soon.

John and Daniel seemed less interested in teasing him, though one day as he walked past them, John said,

"So Charlie, just how tall do you feel today?"

"Tall enough," said Charlie with a smile.

TEN HELPFUL HINTS
FOR PARENTS WHOSE CHILD IS BEING BULLIED

by Dr. Richard Woolfson

1. Always treat complaints of bullying seriously. Remember that it takes a great deal of courage for your child to admit to you that he is being bullied. Reassure him that you will deal with things carefully in a way that protects him.

2. Show that you understand. Let him know that you understand how difficult this is for him to cope with. He needs to feel that you don't think badly of him for complaining.

3. Emphasise that this is now a shared problem which can be solved. Tell him that the problem is solvable, and that you and he will work together on this until the bullying stops.

4. Boost his self-confidence. Help your child feel more positively about himself and his achievements. Remind him of all his good grades in school and emphasise that you think he is marvellous.

5. Persuade him to walk away. He should discretely move away whenever the bully appears to be moving in his direction. This is not an act of cowardice.

6. When confronted, tell him not to react. Ignoring verbal and physical threats is difficult, but it can be done successfully and the bully will stop eventually if he gets no reaction.

7. Don't tell him to fight back. Even if he succeeds, he will think this is an acceptable way for dealing with all sorts of problems in his life.

8. Suggest he stays in a crowd, especially in free time. Bullies pick on children who seem weak and isolated - therefore, a child standing alone in the school playground is easily identified as a potential target.

9. Encourage your child to look assertive and confident, by walking with his shoulders held back, his back upright and his eyes looking directly in front of him, not towards the ground.

10. Speak to school staff. Bullying is most effectively tackled in collaboration with teachers, parents and pupils. However, make it clear that your child should not be publicly identified as the one who complained.

The helping hand books

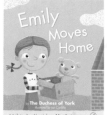

Emily Moves Home
by The Duchess of York
Illustrated by Ian Cunliffe
A helping hand book from Lloydspharmacy

Ben Goes to the Doctor's
and Sophie visits the Dentist
by Sarah, Duchess of York
Illustrated by Ian Cunliffe
A helping hand book from Lloydspharmacy

Simon Gets Better
by Sarah, Duchess of York
Illustrated by Ian Cunliffe
A helping hand book from Lloydspharmacy

Holly's First Day at School
by Sarah, Duchess of York
Illustrated by Ian Cunliffe
A helping hand book from Lloydspharmacy

When Katie's Mum and Dad Separated
by Sarah, Duchess of York
Illustrated by Ian Cunliffe
A helping hand book from Lloydspharmacy

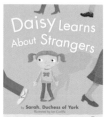

Daisy Learns About Strangers
by Sarah, Duchess of York
Illustrated by Ian Cunliffe
A helping hand book from Lloydspharmacy

Harry Starts to Enjoy His Food
by Sarah, Duchess of York
Illustrated by Ian Cunliffe
A helping hand book from Lloydspharmacy

Dalia Says Goodbye to Grandpa
by Sarah, Duchess of York
A helping hand book from Lloydspharmacy

Jack Takes More Exercise
by Sarah, Duchess of York
Illustrated by Ian Cunliffe
A helping hand book from Lloydspharmacy

Charlie and the Bullies
by Sarah, Duchess of York
Illustrated by Ian Cunliffe
A helping hand book from Lloydspharmacy

Thomas and His New Baby Brother
by Sarah, Duchess of York
Illustrated by Ian Cunliffe
A helping hand book from Lloydspharmacy

Sophie Makes Friends
by Sarah, Duchess of York
Illustrated by Ian Cunliffe
A helping hand book from Lloydspharmacy

Lloydspharmacy